ANIMAL ALLIES

COYOTES AND BADGERS TEAM UP!

BY GLORIA KOSTER

CAPSTONE PRESS
a capstone imprint

Published by Capstone Press, an imprint of Capstone.
1710 Roe Crest Drive, North Mankato, Minnesota 56003
capstonepub.com

Library of Congress Cataloging-in-Publication Data
Names: Koster, Gloria, author.
Title: Coyotes and badgers team up! / by Gloria Koster.
Description: North Mankato, Minnesota : Capstone Press, [2023] | Series: Animal allies | Includes bibliographical references. | Audience: Ages 8 to 11 | Audience: Grades 4-6 | Summary: "Coyotes and badgers team up to hunt prey in this photo-filled nonfiction resource for young wildlife enthusiasts. One cunning coyote + one burrowing badger = a tremendous twosome! Discover how two vastly different animal species team up for a successful hunt. With sharp senses and speed, coyotes are skilled hunters on their own - except when their prey hides underground. Cue the badgers! These mighty diggers claw into rabbit holes and prairie dog burrows, chasing out the hidden prey. And when they do, this dream team feasts! With eye-popping photographs, quick facts, and beyond-the-book back matter, Coyotes and Badgers Team Up! will have young research writers and wildlife fans rooting for these Animal Allies"-- Provided by publisher.
Identifiers: LCCN 2022052690 (print) | LCCN 2022052691 (ebook) | ISBN 9781669048640 (hardcover) | ISBN 9781669048596 (paperback) | ISBN 9781669048602 (ebook PDF) | ISBN 9781669048626 (kindle edition) | ISBN 9781669048633 (epub)
Subjects: LCSH: Coyote--Behavior--Juvenile literature. | Badgers--Behavior--Juvenile literature. | Mutualism (Biology)--Juvenile literature.
Classification: LCC QL737.C22 K79 2023 (print) | LCC QL737.C22 (ebook) | DDC 599.76/7--dc23/eng/20230126
LC record available at https://lccn.loc.gov/2022052690
LC ebook record available at https://lccn.loc.gov/2022052691

Editorial Credits
Editor: Donald Lemke; Designer: Kay Fraser; Media Researcher: Svetlana Zhurkin; Production Specialist: Katy LaVigne

Image Credits
agefotostock: Mary Evans Picture Library Ltd/Tom & Pat Leeson, 17, 20; Alamy: Chris Frost, 26, George Sanker, 24; Dreamstime: Mikael Males, 11, Tamifreed, 13, Teresa Wilson, 29; Getty Images: Jeremy Woodhouse, 9, JohnPitcher, 5, Tom Brakefield, 21, W. Perry Conway, 22 (right); Shutterstock: Dennis Laughlin, 7, Elesey (background), cover, back cover, and throughout, Geoffrey Kuchera, 6, GLF Media, 27, Green Mountain Exposure, 10, Harry Collins Photography, cover (top left), Holly S Cannon, 28, Ken Schulze, cover (bottom), Lev Frid, cover (top right), Lloyd Wallin Photography, 18, Matt Knoth, 4, outdoorsman, 19, slowmotiongli, 22 (left), The Sturdy Table, 12, Tory Kallman, 8, William Dillingham, 25; Superstock: Mary Evans Picture Library/Mary ClayPantheo, 15, 16

Printed and bound in the USA. 5425

Table of Contents

Words in **bold** are in the glossary.

The Invitation

A warm breeze blows across the **prairie** on a summer night. A male coyote is hungry. He leaves his den, where his partner and pups are sleeping. If necessary, the coyote will travel miles to find food.

Tonight, he is lucky. He does not need to travel far. His sharp nose leads him to a prairie dog burrow. But the coyote cannot make the prairie dog leave its hole.

The coyote needs a partner to help him.

A badger is also at home with his family. When the coyote comes calling, the badger leaves his den. He accepts the coyote's invitation.

These two predators compete. They go after the same meal. Still, they like to hunt together. Each has a skill the other does not. Working together increases their odds of finding food. As partners, they succeed more often than when hunting alone.

A coyote and a badger after a hunt

DID YOU KNOW?

Coyotes and badgers can survive in many habitats including grasslands, swamps, marshes, meadows, and deserts. Coyotes can also live in cities and suburbs.

CHAPTER TWO

An Odd Couple

A coyote and a badger are a funny-looking pair. They are so different.

You might mistake a coyote for a wolf or dog. Coyotes, wolves, and dogs are all **canines**. Another name for the coyote is "prairie wolf."

Coyotes have lean bodies. They have black noses and yellow eyes. They have pointy ears on the tops of their heads. Coyote fur is usually gray and brown. It is reddish around their snouts.

Like dogs, coyotes leave a scent. They mark their territory on rocks and grass. This tells other animals where they've been.

Other animals also identify coyotes from their sounds. Coyotes howl, bark, and growl. They make high-pitched yipping sounds. A coyote sound can be a friendly greeting. Other times, it's a signal that danger is close by.

Coyotes are **omnivores**. They eat rabbits and ground squirrels. They go after mice and prairie dogs. Besides mammals, coyotes hunt birds, snakes, and insects. Sometimes they even eat fruits and vegetables. Coyotes are most active at night. But they are not fully **nocturnal**.

A coyote pouncing

Coyotes are smart. They have a sharp sense of smell. Their ears can hear the tiniest sounds. Coyotes can track prey for miles. They like to stalk first. Then they pounce. Coyotes usually work alone. But they sometimes join a pack. This is useful for tracking larger animals like deer. In the summer, the coyote seeks one special partner: the badger.

Badgers are related to skunks and otters. They are members of the **weasel** family.

Badgers have short legs and necks. They have wide heads. Badgers are covered in gray fur. A white stripe runs from a badger's back to its nose. Badgers have lower jaws that stick out. This helps them firmly grip their prey. They also have sharp teeth.

Badgers have webbed front feet. Their front claws are curved. Their back claws act like shovels. They use their feet to dig into burrows. This is how badgers capture their prey.

A badger shows its sharp teeth and long claws.

Badgers spend the winter underground. They do not hibernate. However, they are less active. During this time, they mostly live off their own fat. When warm weather returns, they are hungry. They are eager to hunt again.

Badgers are nocturnal. They usually go out at night. Like coyotes, badgers are omnivores. In fact, these two animals have the same diet.

DID YOU KNOW?

Badgers live together in a community. Their dens are called setts. Badger setts are made up of many underground tunnels. Setts are passed along from one generation to the next. Inside their setts, badgers are very clean. They regularly change the leaves and grass they use for their beds.

A badger and coyote walk near each other in
Yellowstone National Park.

Coyotes and badgers are both skilled hunters.
They each go after the same prey. So why aren't
they enemies?

Scientists don't know when the unusual
relationship began. But at some point, coyotes and
badgers began to **collaborate**.

CHAPTER THREE

The Hunt

When a coyote and a badger hunt together, they each play a part. The coyote takes the lead. Its sharp nose tells it where to go. If the prey is underground, the coyote needs help. Alone, it cannot grab a creature hidden in a burrow.

Outside the badger's den, the coyote wags its tail. It bows down. It looks like a dog wanting to play. This gets the badger's attention. It recognizes this invitation and comes out of its hole.

The partners do not walk side by side. The badger is slower. It raises its tail. It **waddles** behind the coyote. The hunt is on!

DID YOU KNOW?

In many Native American legends, coyotes play tricks on other animals. Badger characters appear in some popular children's books, including *The Wind in the Willows* and *Fantastic Mr. Fox*.

A coyote and badger hunt near a burrow.

The coyote and badger arrive at their target. Some nights it's a rabbit hole. Other times it's the home of a mouse, ground squirrel, or prairie dog. There is often more than one entrance. The coyote stands guard at one of the openings. At another entrance, the badger starts digging.

DID YOU KNOW?

Badgers dig quickly. This produces a cloud of dirt. Special eyelids protect their eyes from the dirt.

Who will get the prairie dog? Will it be the coyote? Will it be the badger? When these partners team up, two things can happen.

The badger's digging may frighten the prairie dog. It may flee from its den. If this happens, it cannot escape the waiting coyote. But if the prairie dog stays underground, the badger will grab it. Either way, the unlucky animal doesn't stand a chance. The two predators are a mighty force!

A coyote waits while a badger digs into a burrow.

A badger captures a praire dog in Badlands National Park, South Dakota.

Sometimes the coyote gets the prey. Sometimes it's the badger. The winner does not share the meal. But the partners usually do not fight. They seem to accept the rule that the winner takes all.

At times, the coyote and badger might both be winners. This could happen if several animals are underground. One might come out of the hole. It will land in the coyote's mouth. Another might stay underground. It won't escape the badger's jaws.

A coyote steals prey from a badger.

CHAPTER FOUR

A Working Relationship

Coyotes and badgers are not actual friends. They are more like friendly coworkers.

When they hunt, they act like a tag team. Hunting together saves energy. With a badger's help, a coyote does better than hunting alone. How much better? A coyote's success increases by about 30 percent. No wonder it likes this partnership!

A coyote and badger hunt together in a prairie dog colony.

A coyote chases a raccoon.

Of course, coyotes can count on badgers only at
certain times. Badgers are not always available in the
daytime. In winter, they do not need coyotes at all.
That's when badgers remain underground. They require
little food. If they happen to get hungry, they can find a
meal. Hibernating animals become easy prey.

In school, students collaborate with classmates. Some group projects may require a product. But different students have different abilities. Combining these abilities can make a product even better. The same is true for coyotes and badgers. They each benefit from the other's strengths.

Coyotes and badgers shine in different ways. Coyotes are fast. They can run 40 miles (64 kilometers) per hour. Coyotes travel across land and water. Besides their speed, they have a powerful sense of smell. Their vision is not as good as most human's. But coyotes have amazing **peripheral vision**. This means they can see out of the corners of their eyes.

Badgers also have good hearing and sense of smell. But they have very poor eyesight. Their bodies are heavy. Compared to coyotes, they move slowly. Their top speed is about 18 miles (29 km) per hour. A rodent can easily escape a badger. But the badger is fantastic at digging. It can dive into small underground spaces. This is a skill the coyote does not have. The coyote can lead its partner to the prey. Then the badger must take over.

In nature, members of two different species may connect. Their connection is called **symbiosis**. Symbiosis may be good for one animal but harmful to the other. But other times, symbiosis is good for both species. This type of symbiosis is called **mutualism**. The partnership between coyotes and badgers is an example of mutualism.

DID YOU KNOW?

Coyotes can outrun their prey, but during a chase, smaller animals can duck into holes. This is when badgers are called into action.

CHAPTER FIVE

Predator or Prey?

Coyotes and badgers are both **aggressive**. They have few predators. However, wolves, bears, and wild cats may attack them. Alligators and golden eagles also spell trouble.

Coyotes can hunt alongside larger animals like wolves. They may not be able to compete for food. They may starve to death.

A wolf and a coyote near each other in the wild.

COLORADO PARKS & WILDLIFE

Coyotes Are Active In This Area

Coyotes in populated areas are typically less fearful of people. They have been known to attack pets and approach people too closely. Please read and share these tips with your children.

If a Coyote Approaches You:
- Do not run or turn your back
- Be as big and loud as possible
- Wave your arms and throw objects
- Face the coyote and back away slowly
- If attacked, fight back

Protect Your Pets:
- Keep pets on a short leash
- Use extra caution dusk through dawn
- Avoid known or potential den sites and thick vegetation
- Do not allow dogs to interact with coyotes

Be Prepared!
If You Have Concerns About an Encounter With A Coyote:
- Recreate during daylight hours
- Walk with a walking stick
- Keep a deterrent spray handy
- Carry noise makers or rocks to throw

Call your local Colorado Parks & Wildlife office or its Denver headquarters at 303-291-7227 or visit cpw.state.co.us to learn more about coyotes.

A sign in a public park warns people about wild coyotes.

Coyotes rarely attack humans, but they may kill cats and dogs. Because they attack sheep and cows, farmers view them as pests. When pets or farm animals are killed, some people shoot coyotes.

Badger holes are very dangerous for horses and cattle. Some dogs are trained to go after badgers. Dachshunds have pointy snouts. This helps them pull badgers from their dens.

A dachshund enters a badger hole.

DID YOU KNOW?

Wolves are not always a danger to coyotes. Sometimes a coyote will breed with a wolf. This produces an animal called a *coywolf*.

A wildlife corridor crosses over a busy highway.

Coyotes and badgers can be hit by automobiles. Roads and highways are dangerous. So are fences and construction sites. It is important to protect wildlife from human development. In some places there are **wildlife corridors**. These pathways help animals move from place to place. There are video cameras inside some of these pathways. Images show coyotes and badgers traveling safely together.

THE COYOTE

Also Known As: Prairie Wolf, Brush Wolf, Song Dog

Species: *Canis latrans*; family includes dogs, wolves, and jackals

Size: About 2 feet (.6 meters) tall; 3–4 feet (.9–1.2 m) long from nose to tail

Weight: 20–50 pounds (9–22.7 kilograms)

Fur: Thick, grayish-brown, bushy tail

Features: Yellow eyes, pointy ears

Pack Size: 3–7

As a Hunting Ally: Stalks prey and then pounces upon it; allows a badger to flush out prey from burrows.

THE BADGER

Also Known As: Brock

Species: *Taxidea taxus*; family includes wolverines, ferrets, and weasels

Size: 9 inches (22.9 centimeters) tall; about 35 inches (89 cm) long

Weight: 9–26 pounds (4–11.8 kg)

Fur: Yellowish-gray, white stripe from nose to back

Features: Thick, short legs and neck, flat head and body, sharp claws

Community Size: Several males and females

As a Hunting Ally: Follows a coyote to prey, digs into burrows, scares prey into leaving home.

Glossary

aggressive (uh-GRESS-iv)—behaving in a way that aims to attack or harm another being

canine (KAY-nyne)—family of mammals that includes dogs, wolves, foxes, and coyotes

collaborate (kuh-LAB-uh-rayt)—to work with others to complete a task

mutualism (MYOO-chuh-liz-um)—the kind of symbiosis that is good for both living things

nocturnal (nahk-TER-nuhl)—active at night

omnivore (AHM-nih-vore)—an animal that eats both plants and animals

peripheral vision (puh-RIF-uh-ruhl VIZH-uhn)—seeing with the corners of our eyes to view things that are not directly in front of us

prairie (PRAYR-ee)—flatland covered mostly with grasses

symbiosis (sim-BYE-oh-siss)—the close relationship between two or more living things

waddle (WAHD-uhl)—to take short steps while also swaying from side to side

weasel (WEE-zuhl)—a small furry mammal with a flat body and short legs

wildlife corridor (WYLD-lyfe CORR-uh-dor)—a tunnel or other passage that connects two areas of land

Read More

Murphy, Macken. *Animal Sidekicks: Amazing Stories of Symbiosis in Animals and Plants.* New York: Macmillan, 2022.

Ruby, Rex. *Inside a Badger's Burrow.* Minneapolis: Bearport Publishing, 2022.

Ward, Jennifer. *Just You and Me: Remarkable Relationships in the Wild.* New York: Simon & Schuster, 2021.

Internet Sites

A-Z Animals: All Animals A–Z List
a-z-animals.com/animals

National Geographic: "Why this Coyote and Badger 'Friendship' Has Excited Scientists"
nationalgeographic.com/animals/article/coyote-badger-video-behavior-friends

Smithsonian Magazine: "Watch a Coyote and Badger Hunt Their Prey Together"
smithsonianmag.com/smart-news/watch-coyote-and-badger-hunt-their-prey-together-1-180974170

Index

About the Author

A public and school librarian, Gloria Koster belongs to the Children's Book Committee of Bank Street College of Education. She enjoys both city and country life, dividing her time between Manhattan and the small town of Pound Ridge, New York. Gloria has three adult children and a bunch of energetic grandkids.